FRIDAY'S COMING

Robert W. Castello

FRIDAY'S COMING

DOUBLE DRAGON

1 - Tears of an Angel

In all of the greater Boston Metro Area, indeed in all of the city of East New England there wasn't a bigger asshole than Lenny Bosco. And now he was dead. And I had killed him. And it turned out that he was a cop.

The moment his heart stopped, the monitor implant sent out the alert "Officer Down" on all freeks and all bands. Every cop in the city knew who and where. Civilians who cared to check the tone would know, and had I bothered to check mine I would have known too. But even as Boston's Finest were converging on the building I had my hands full trying to siphon what Angel Tears I could from the port in the man's brain.

Lenny had always been a real jerk. He was a Touch-Head and an easy mark. When I couldn't score tears from heads at the usual clubs he was my fallback. He liked my body and his price was just a giggle dance. I didn't mind that. What I hated was his attitude. He would lord over me like he was a somebody, and he'd have me dance down to my slippery pretties while he got a bone on and used his toy to get off, right there in front of me.

It was pretty gross, but it would stimulate his brain. Capillaries would flush and the path down the port would be so much easier. I could always easily get a quarter dram from the man and we'd both be happy.

But that night he'd been drinking more than usual. He took a long time to climax and he was squirrely. I saw that and I should have stepped away. But I was pissed. I'd worked for the fix and I wasn't going to go away empty.

I slammed him into a chair. I should have tied him up or something, but by that time I was hurting. I parted his hair and found the port on the crown of his head. I worked him from behind as I started the probe. He giggled.

"Don't move," I said.

"Yes Ma'am."

"I mean it and you know it."

My micro tube followed the wire lead. It was all touch and feel, but I'd done that so many, many times and I knew my way around Lenny's brain. The probe glided smoothly centimeter by centimeter, deep into the grey.

"Almost home, baby," I said.

"Oh, baby."

That should have tipped me. My wrists were resting on his head as I worked. I hit a snag. I had to draw the thing back a little and then go forward a couple of times. I was getting frustrated. I hadn't realized that my boobs were cradling his head. I felt him shudder, but I didn't see his hand creeping up. I finally got past the hitch and the probe slid straight into the sack.

Deep in the center of his brain, nestled comfortably in the nucleus accumbens there was a micro implant. A wire threaded through the grey matter to a port on the surface of the skull. When that port was plugged into an Angel he'd get a trickle of micro-amps, the massaging would start and his touch-head brain would be bathed in dopamine sending him into euphoria.

6

The beauty side was that, beyond the initial operation, there were no physical harms to the body. There was no liver pickling, no lungs rotting, no chance of an overdose. It was an addict's dream.

The down side was that a byproduct fluid would build up around the implant. Held in a sack by surface tension, the buildup was microscopic and harmless --unless it built up too much and the sack ruptured. That would be very bad for the brain. The upside was that the fluid was easily removed, and the liquid was itself gold for the biotechs.

For me, the stuff was life.

But this time it was death.

I had just begun drawing the tears when the idiot started stroking my tit. I jerked. The siphon responded and the sack ruptured. The next thing I knew Lenny was on the floor convulsing, my precious tears seeping into his hair. I wanted to scream.

I was on him like that. There was no more need for care or caution. The guy was already dead. Moments after the blood flow stopped the brain would collapse in a cascade. I reattached the syringe and drew the plunger. I got a full dram, but there was a lot of blood in there. At that point I didn't care. I needed to get out of there. That's when I heard the sirens.

By then it was too late.

Two of them burst in through the window. Six busted down the door. I was surrounded by Blue in armor. Eight guns were cocked and pointed at me. Before I knew what was happening something slammed into my kidneys, and I was down on my face, wrists cuffed, palms out, thumbs up. There was a lot of shouting and very bad language. E-Meds were all over Lenny.

I was frantic. The syringe lay on the floor within my sight and there were boots everywhere. Someone's heel glanced the thing and it skidded to the wall. I shrieked and thrashed. I felt a muzzle to my head as I gazed at the precious tears.

"Quit your bitching, whore," someone shouted.

The gun barrel near twisted my neck.

"You don't understand," I cried.

For that I got a boot in the ribs.

"He's gone," an E-Med said.

"You're fucked, bitch."

I knew that was the truth. Before I would ever see a jail or a judge they'd have a time with me. Maybe they'd take me someplace or maybe they'd do me right there, but the fact was that I'd killed one of theirs and they really didn't like that. Or me.

"You don't understand," I managed.

"Sure, I understand," someone said. "Stand her up."

A hand grabbed me by the hair, twisting my head. I was pulled to my feet. I teetered in my heels as I faced the head cop. He was chubby, ugly and had no hair. He had a face that was all lines and folds and dark eyes. He wore a good suit and he smelled of lousy cologne. The anger on his face started to melt into a grin.

"What's your name?" he asked.

"Martha Stewart."

"That's a lie. But no matter. We'll figure you out soon enough."

8

A light flashed in my eyes. They had my retina.

"So here's the way I understand things," chubby went on. "My friend Lenny was a touch-head. You're a gleaner. You want the angel-tears. You two meet, set things up and something went wrong. Am I right so far?"

"Yeah."

"So what went wrong?"

"I was stupid," I said. I clutched to the hope that the man was reasonable. "Lenny was drunk. I shouldn't have dove in."

"But you did," he said. "You that desperate?"

"Getting there."

"Go on."

"The perv—sorry --Lenny grabbed me. I twitched. I didn't mean to. My siphon—"

"Yeah," he said. "I get it. Accident. Still manslaughter."

"And a cop," one of the others said.

"And a cop," boss man repeated. "Bosco had a family, didn't he?"

"Yeah. Partner and two kids."

"Jeeze what a shame. Kids growing up without a father and all."

"And without an income," the other added. "Insurance finds out he was a touch-head they're gonna laugh at any claim."

"Man that's tough."

'It was his own damned fault,' I wanted to say. But in the middle of nine cops and eight guns what I said was,

"Look, I'm sorry. It was an accident. What can I do, to help make things better?"

9

Boss man's grin widened.

"Pretty thing like you can do a lot," he said. "In fact I know a place where you can make things so much better. Healthy young girl like you can get those kids through college."

"I think I'd rather take my chances with a judge," I said.

Boss man started to chuckle. The others joined him.

"My car," he said.

They started to hustle me away.

"Please," I cried. "My tears. I need my tears. If I die on you I won't be making anything for anyone."

"Oh you'll get your tears, missy," he said, grabbing up the syringe. "You'll get plenty of tears." Then he motioned to Lenny. "You boys know what to do with Bosco. Meet us at the garage; get your share before we put pretty Miss Martha to work."

"Bastards," I spat.

That's when the groping started. I tried desperately not to panic. My mind raced. I knew that if I ever got in their car I'd never see the daylight again. There were four of them escorting me. Their weapons were holstered but I was still outnumbered.

In the elevator the boss and his buddy slammed me into the back wall. They were all over me, pawing and mauling and laughing, but as it turned out that was the only lucky thing that happened to me that night. The two cops in front were turned and watching. So when the doors opened to the lobby they didn't see the two blazers. The green

10

bolts ripped through their cop armor and their chests exploded.

I didn't think. I kneed boss man in the pills and he crumbled. On his way down I kicked his jaw. I think he sliced his tongue. The other had his hand under my panties and on my ass. He lost his head.

I was grabbed by two figures in the door. They were in dazzle-mail head to toe; rings of tungsten with a charge that made them sparkle. They literally carried me across the lobby and away out the doors. A crowd had gathered around the cop-car. The dead driver was sprawled on the sidewalk. They threw me inside and a third drove.

We rose like a shot straight up to the Emergency-Lane, lights flashing and sirens wailing. A bullet tore through the back window. My dazzle-knights immediately punched through the inner doors and grabbed the outer shell. Their charge surrounded the car and I heard no more bullets hit. The driver raced down the lane. I looked behind. Three cop cars were following. We were heading out over the harbor. I looked ahead. There were two big Border Flyers banking to intercept us.

I figured that at least I wouldn't die in some whorehouse.

And then the driver pulled the oldest trick in the book. He slammed on the breaks and we dropped like a stone. The cops flew past us. We just missed a bus in the commuter lane as we plunged. We kept falling. We hit the harbor. The charge surrounding the car vaporized the water and we were engulfed in white spume. Then my knights let go the hull. The car flooded quickly and we sank.

As I took my last deep breath one of my knights broke the window with his elbow. We swam out as the car plunged down the murky depths. Their dazzle-mail was still charged and so repelled water. We swam at a dizzying speed. And as my lungs were about to give out we broke the surface.

I gasped and drank in air. My head was spinning. Literally. The muscles in my spinal cord were enflamed. I'd lost my fix and my own body was beginning to strangle my nervous system, and it didn't help that my hands were still cop-cuffed. My shoulder blades were cramped and pressing.

About a mile away the cops and border flyers were hovering over our crash site. My silent knights swam. Then I heard old-style chugging. We came up on a lobster boat. I was hauled aboard. I lay half astonished among the traps and crustaceans while one knight spoke with the boater. It wasn't long before I was wrapped in clean blankets.

One of the knights dried my face and the bald side of my head. Then he stuck a transponder in my ear. He kissed his fingers and placed them on my lips. And if a man in a suit of dazzle-mail could wink I swore he did. Then he left my sight and I heard splashes.

"Jenny?"

The sound in my ear was like an explosion.

"Whaaa?" I gasped.

"Jessica Teasdale," he said. "You oksy?"

"No!"

"Are you in a whore house?"

"No."

"Then you're ok."

12

"Alistair?"

"Yepper."

"What the flup is all this?"

"I need you baby."

"Your dazzlers killed three cops."

"Eight," he said, chuckling. "We took out the ones in the room. Big flash bang. You shoulda seen."

"Alistair," I almost shouted. "You can't kill cops."

"I can."

"What the flup?"

"Cops are as cross as Angels."

"Speaking of which," I said.

"I know baby," he said. "You lost your dose."

"Damn it Alistair! I lost my dose, I lost my kit, I lost my dress and I lost my purse!"

"You break a fingernail?"

"Alistair! I need—"

"You need to stay calm. I got you this far. I'll get you home."

"What good will that do? They took a shot of my eyes."

"Silly girl," he said. "That's how I found your needy ass years ago."

"I don't flupping believe this."

"Believe what you will," he said. "You've had a long night. You're tense. Sleep now. Trust the old lobster-man. In a few days I am going to need you."

"Alistair!"

"Sleep baby."

"I so hate you."

The earpiece started to buzz. I didn't fight it. The vibrations put me to sleep.

2 - Alistair

When I woke I was in my own bed. The walls of my house were still sound and that was a good thing. But for the small soft scent of the harbor water in my hair there was no evidence of the night's adventure. I was naked and I could move my hands. The marks from the cuffs were ugly. I rolled over and felt something warm and soft.

"Geena?"

"Yes mistress," my slave said. "Feeling oksy?"

"What happened?"

"There was a delivery truck yesterday," she said. "They had your codes. They brought you in. Got a couple of nice lobsters too. You going to live?"

I thought about that. My spine was relaxed. The tension was gone. I could breathe. Somehow, sometime someone had dosed me.

"Yeah," I said. "What time is it?"

"Morning. Sunday."

I thought about that. It was Friday night when Bosco and I hooked up. I'd been out a full day.

"I was frightened for you," Geena said.

"Can you do that?"

"I can," she said,

"Do tell."

"It's self-preservation," Geena said, stroking my eyebrow. "I've been with you over two years. I consider myself lucky. You're nice. I like it here. If something were to happen to you I would have go back to the Farm, and the possibility of being sold

15

to someone not so nice is very real. So yes, mistress, I was afraid."

"Cool," I smiled. "So how about showing some appreciation?"

"Happily, mistress."

The things that cyborg could do.

Breakfast, however, was not one of them. I learned that long ago. I cooked while Geena caught me up on my calls.

Six were from Roger. We had a date Saturday night. His first call was irritated. The next two were concerned. The last ones were pissed. I shrugged it off. He wasn't that special.

I had one call from my accountant begging me to get back to him.

Then there was one from the pool service. They had a schedule snafu and wanted to come by that Tuesday instead of Thursday. I blew that one off too.

Then Geena twitched.

"Incoming – restricted," she said and rattled off a number.

"Hang on," I said.

I went to the gate panel and dialed the code for the shield. I couldn't have any spying on this one. I went back to my coffee.

"Take it," I said.

She sat across from me at the table. Her face shimmered, and then her head morphed into the likeness of Alistair. Alistair was an older man with a lean, grandfatherly face and silver hair. He was rugged and worn. He had been a career active

Colonial Marine. A drunk driver clipped his flyer and sent him into retirement. He worked for some shadowy Intel agency. And I worked for him. Seeing his face superimposed on Geena's luscious body was a hoot.

"You look good with tits," I said.

"You look better with them," he answered.

"Where are you?"

"That's classified."

"Okay, what's up?"

"This."

Geena's hand waved and an image appeared on the table. They were two girls. They were twins. They had young, oval faces with high cheekbones and long thin noses. Their eyes were round and yet almost oriental the way they slanted slightly and had that fold on the inside. They wore thick liner, upper and lower so that I wondered if they might be tattooed. But they had soft, arching eyebrows. Two of them. Over each eye. They had blue lips that shaded deep in the center so that they looked like they were puckering up for a kiss. Their rich auburn hair was long and silky with slender metallic blue braids framing. And peeping from their temples they had tiny faun horns.

"Cute," I said. "Who are they?"

"Meet Jane and Jane Rozlapa," he said. "Twins."

"Jane and Jane? Their parent not so creative?"

"I have no idea. All I know is that they are in the city and they want to get to Latvia. I want them."

"Why?"

"They're wanted for murder in two provinces," he said. "They're dangerous. Cops, Feds, Marines, even Emigration are looking for them."

"They don't look like the murdering type."

"And what is the murdering type supposed to look like?"

"Point taken," I said. "So how am I supposed to find them?"

"They'll try and find a smuggler, and Bean-Town is prime. That's your department."

"It's a big department," I said. "Lots of ships pass through. I see a fraction."

"Well then," he said, "you're going to have to figure out how to see more. This is a big one. You score this for me and you're going to be that much closer to Friday."

"You say that a lot."

"I mean it, sweetie."

Geena's hand reached under her shirt and pulled out a crystal vial. The clear liquid gleamed. I caught my breath. Without thinking I reached for the thing, but my fingers found only air.

"No more angel tears," he said. "I want those girls."

"You're a son of a bitch."

"You've said that," he smiled placing the vial back under Geena's shirt. "Now here's the catch. I don't care how you snag 'em, but under no circumstances are they to be drugged. You got that? No dope. I want 'em clean."

"What if I can't find them?"

The image on the table vanished, and a mug shot appeared. He was bald, hairless and ugly.

18

"This is Detective Sergeant Adolpho of the city's finest. He's got a grudgey with you."

"You're a—"

"I know. I'm a son of a bitch. But that's how important this is. When you snag 'em you call me immediately. You need help, you call. You don't need help, you call. I want regular updates. I want—"

"You want, you want, you want," I said, seething. "How the hell am I supposed to move? Your boys put a dent in the cop-shop the other night and the only lead they have is me."

"Don't be so stupid. Cops are looking for Jessica Teasdale. I'm hiring Samantha Waters."

I sat fuming.

"Hang in there baby," he said as his face began to flicker. "Friday's coming."

3 - Samantha

Samantha Waters was an administrative agent at the city of Boston's Bureau of Customs and Inspections. She was my height, my build, my coloring and, with a little finagling, my retina pattern. I never knew why she disappeared. She went off on holiday one week, and I came back in her place. It was supposed to be a temporary thing. Alistair wanted to snag a ring of smugglers trading in Nasty. Samantha was very crooked and so I was put in there as her. I cooperated on the promise of my Friday.

I am a survivor of the Uptown Fever. The name was a misnomer, really; Uptown Fever was a whole host of crap that rampaged through Uptown Town on the L-2 colony. The main part was a virus that caused fever that could fry your brain. It also had a whole bunch of other fun stuff that went along for the ride, like uncontrollable bleeding from all sorts of fun places. There was no treatment and no cure.

Some of us just sweated it out and survived, but there was damage from being so hot for so long. My primary motor cortex went hinkie. Every few weeks, with a pattern that was almost as predictable as my period, muscles in my back would slowly swell and strangle my spinal cord. Angel tears would set things right, for a while. A dose of Frinalolchoday would cure it; Friday.

I had a host of remedies for the loneliness of menstruation.

Only tears or my Friday would keep me alive.

And so, of course, that was the hook. Alistair claimed that I was on a sort of point system. I did his dirty work and came ever closer to salvation. But I never knew just where I was on his scale, nor did I know how close each job got me. And so every Monday morning Samantha Waters would smile and log in to work.

"Make-over time, Mistress?" Geena asked.

Her face came back. She looked a little drained as she always did after a call like that.

"I guess," I sighed. "And I so wanted to relax."

"It won't take long. Then you and Samantha can relax. I'll meet you at the chair."

I hated that part. The chair that would clamp my head. Then Geena would mist my eyes with a muscle relaxant. My vision was locked starting straight. Then came the pupil dilators and that was the worst. As my irises expanded and my vision went all blurry, I couldn't focus, I could hardly feel anything in my eyes, and yet I knew exactly what was going on.

Geena would peel aside my cornea, pop out my lens, and then with my pupil open to the world she's slip in the little membrane that would conform to my retina like a decal. There were these teeny-tiny little alignment marks that she had to line up perfect. The whole time I saw blurry images of the hair thin tools. Then she'd put everything back together and go do the other eye. Then I'd have to lay there for two hours, bandaged and still.

I could have had the procedure done once and have had an end to it. But Alistair insisted that if I went out gleaning tears as Samantha and got caught, like I did that night, he'd let me twist. Samantha Waters would be gone and so would her cushy house in the gated Chelsea burbs. So every few weeks or so Samantha and Jessica would trade places, and back again.

Bright and early that Monday morning I sprayed on my lovely blonde wig, tied it up in a bun, dressed in my Bureau armor and boots, kissed my slave goodbye, grabbed my purse and flagged the bus to work.

The tower port on my house had a lovely view of the filthy river. On one side I could look on the Navy Yards, all spit and polish and bristling with order. Across the river in Eagle Hills it looked like a nice day; I counted only four fires raging in Hell-town. Beyond that the crater that was once Logan airport was littered with shanties and tents.

The flight to the Customs House in the middle of Cape Cod Bay was uneventful. Morning traffic in the authorized lane was brisk but clipped along. Below in the commuter lane it was beginning to look like a hover lot, and I couldn't help thinking about that waste of energy. As soon as we past the Winthrop Toll we were almost alone in the air and we boogied. Most of us on the shuttle knew each other and the chatter was always light. People talked about the lottery, the Red Sox and the weather. Nobody talked about work; that would come on Wednesday when the bitching would begin.

"Sam," a cheery voice cried. "Sam, guess what?"

"Hey, Charlotte," I smiled. "You passed your prelims."

"I did, I did!" she said grabbing a seat next to me. "I got the wave soon as I got home Friday. I wanted to call you but you were flagged unavailable. You have a time this weekend?"

I was a sort of mentor to the girl. She was fresh out of Amherst and working on the docks. I'd see her a lot during my inspections and sometimes I'd tag her for a search team. She really wanted to be an agent, and I was sort of helping her. Her first hurdle was to spend a few years as an inspector.

"To be honest," I said, "I don't remember a lot of it."

She giggled.

"So anyway," I said. "What did you score?"

"Eighty-eight."

"That good," I nodded. "Good enough to get you in to One-oh-One."

"I placed out of that," she said. "My grades. I start on Schematics next week."

"Oh you are gonna just love that."

"I can't wait. It's eight weeks and for my final I get to lead a search, and I get real armor."

"Sometimes I think you only want the job for the suit."

"It is a cute suit."

Cute was not the word I'd have chosen; more like form-fitting. But it had to be. Smugglers are brilliant, and getting smarter and you have to be able to slip, literally, through some of the tightest places. The shark-skin has a sort of Teflon coat and doesn't snag. It also has power points that zip you up in dazzle-mail if things get rough; helmet included. If things get rougher it can lock you into a

23

stasis cocoon. The downside was that you walked around like somebody had sprayed you with navy blue. I always wore a skirt over, but everyone still checked out my boobs all the time.

"Yeah," I said. "It is. Look good on you too."

"I can't wait."

So for the rest of the flight she pumped me for info about her class and I promised that I'd help her cheat however I could. She was becoming like my little sister.

My Monday was like any Monday; chatter around the coffee machine, sit in my office and pretend to plan, check out the manifests, stuff like that. But that Monday I had to figure out how the hell I was going to track down a pair of homicidal teenage twins.

The Custom House was a sprawling spider of a port in the bay. We handled ocean traffic slogging into Boston and we took in smaller off-world rigs. Those little boats would usually crew three or four and carry less than 500 tons. My job was to look for anything weird and go sniffing.

Pretty much anyone who wanted to smuggle bodies would use a little ship. If they were going off-planet they'd only have to hide at the Ports: the time between could be long and nobody wanted to stay in a coffin or something that long. Despite Sci-Fi dreamers nobody had yet to figure out hibernation, and stasis suits were, to say the least expensive.

But my girls wanted to go to Latvia. Commercial air was out for them and an ocean trip, even in a sub

24

would have taken forever; and that's a lot of food and TP. After some digging I figured that a little-ship could get them from Boston to Riga in less than ninety minutes. I had to start somewhere.

I listed the inbound littles. There were two corporate, two yachts, one single-ship, a rig from Nurses-Without-Boundaries and three private cargo ships. Two of the cargos had passenger accommodations. I flagged them all. I had a hunch about the Nurses, but then when I saw the crews I smiled.

I rode up to the landing pallet. The view of the cape and the ocean was spectacular. In the bright haze I saw the ocean side fading from brown to green. There were actual white whitecaps way out. It was so beautiful. In the pilot's lounge I had a bunch of angry people. But they were smart enough not to piss me off.

"Cookie," I smiled when I saw my man.

Captain Nathan Cook was a character, a charmer and a brazen smuggler. He dressed half as an ancient Highland warrior and half as a gentleman at afternoon tea. He wore good yak-leather knee high combat boots with white spats and tassels. His pleated kilt was blue alligator skin and the sporran that hung over his crotch was of woven metal beads. He wore a white shirt with a stiff-kitty, red bow tie and a navy blue double breasted morning coat, sans tails. His long braided hair was the color of wet beach sand and yet his scruff of a beard was red. He had a face that looked like it had been crafted, and a smile that looked like he had a secret.

And Nathan Cook always had a secret.

I was fifty-fifty with the man. I'd catch him half the time, but every time he made me happy. I'd have to fine him on occasion to keep thing good with my bosses, and he never tried to sneak Nasties. He'd always have a legit cargo that wasn't worth the price of fuel and so it was my game to figure what he was hiding. One time it was cow embryos, and another time it was prom gowns woven of Crease gel-silk taxed at triple their worth.

"Sammie," he said with a smile. "You are looking lovely as ever. What's up on this end? You got a lotta boats locked up. Something brewing?"

"I dunno," I said. "Nothing's perishable so I want to have a look see."

"The Nurses have perishables."

"The Nurses have refrigerators. Let's go check your samples."

"Okie-dokie."

His ship was docked in orbit at Up-Port Nine. He had a standard hold loaded and in compliance, and so the pickers grabbed random samples, sealed and loaded them onto his lander and sent him to the Custom House.

"What do we got here, Cookie?"

His lander was a real custom job. It was a three seater, a long orca-tube number with gently rounded stingray wings and twin turbojet engines. He had it painted with the wavy black and white pattern of the killer shark. The thing could make it to Riga easy.

"Star-shine," he said. "Like the labels say. One hundred-proof, knock you blind star-shine. I got a case complimentary so if you'd like—"

"Are you trying to bribe me?"

"Always."

"Okay. What else you got?"

"My word," he said. "Nothing here."

"What do you got upstairs?"

"My word," he said again. "Five hundred half-liter cases of star-shine. Dyed green and all wanting to be in Bean-town for the Saint Pat's Day. It's a time sensitive load, you understand."

"It's always time sensitive with you."

I snooped. I needed an excuse. His shuttle was spotless, and that was always a sign. I scanned the cargo. Nothing. Then I scanned the cockpit. It was a three-seater and the second seat was pristine. It smelled of a wipe-down.

"You drive this thing down yourself?" I asked.

"When I have to."

"You had to?"

"My co-pilot is sick," he said shaking his head. "She has cramps. It's kind of embarrassing but --- well, you know."

"Yeah I do," I said. "I know what muscle cramping can do, and I know that there are a dozen ways to ease it. So your co-pilot has been living in the dark, she's stupid or you're lying about something."

"Now wait—"

"Now I can quarantine this vessel and this platform or . . ."

"What?"

"You and me go see the *May Queen*," I said. "I want to check out your ship."

"So I gotta say—"

"Say it upstairs. We'll take my car"

27

It took me two hours to clear the paperwork and requisition a ship. I got a real zoomer; a small four passenger blind needle-ship, something like the back end of a narrow wasp. It was a honey. I grabbed my kit, my purse and Cook. Flight clearance took almost another hour. We saw nothing of the ride after we blasted, but we were docking on his ship inside of fifteen minutes.

The *May Queen* was colony rated. It could land anywhere but Earth. It was a clunky looking thing. It was a tube with a bulb snout, retractable x-wing solar panels, a standard doughnut living section amidships and a hulking plasma-ion drive. In real inter-colony flight the motor needed to trail the main body by a mile. Radiation. At the station the thing was cold and all tucked up neat. My needle-ship slipped nicely into his docking station. Nothing was rotating, so that meant freefall. I figured that whiskey didn't need gravity. Neither did whatever he was smuggling.

"The cargo is forward," he said as we floated through the airlock. "Where it always is."

"I want to see the living space first."

"Okie-dokie."

I never could understand how people could get used to round walls. I like boxes. I like things level and square. The doughnut had a central corridor and several rooms on either side. The lights were dim. The man was saving power.

"Where's the crew?" I asked scanning the place. "I got no signs of bodies."

"Probably out at Mickey's getting drunk," he said. "We got station passes."

"Cool. Let's go look at the parlor."

"Right this way, M'Lady."

We worked our way along the handholds. The place smelled of burnt almonds. At some point in the very recent past he had blown out all the air to space.

Humans have a cloud of garbage hovering around them; bacteria, dander, bits of belches, farts, coughs and sneezes, and the mist is like a signature. So he'd dumped his air to get rid of something.

The parlor was a typical rec-room. They had a wide-field holo, card table, stereo and the like. The snooker table told me that he flew with the living space spinning. The balls needed gravity. I floated to the wall near the table. I scanned at about crotch height. I smiled. Somebody had ripped a good one.

"So," I said. "You had something to say?"

"I do," he said nodding. "This way."

We floated to the kitchen and into the walk-in pantry. He shut the door. It was his safe place. It was shielded and so nobody down at the Custom House or on the station could hear anything from my suit.

"Shit it's freezing in here," I said.

"I got perishables," he said.

"You got people," I said showing him my scan. "That's FCB, and it don't match your crew's DNA."

Wherever you find mammals you're going to find fecal coli-form bacteria. You wipe your ass, you wash your hands, you don't get everything. You touch the wall and the transfer starts to grow a cute little colony. You pass gas and the little

29

beasties settle and grow. Bacteria, like people, want things warm.

"Somebody leaned against the wall," I said. "They farted. I get a female from my scan. She's preggers, and she don't match your co-pilot. So tell me what you got."

"I got fifty large for you," he said. "Coin or slivers. Your choice."

Fifty was a nice sum. After I paid off my people I'd still have had a good day. But I needed more.

"You're coming from Vesta," I said. "There's been trouble there. You got felons?"

"Everybody there's a felon these days," he said chuckling. "Hell, on Stratumus you can get two years for jay-walking. I can go to sixty five."

He could probably have gone to seventy-five.

"Here's the deal," I said.

I took my phone from my purse. I called up the image Alistair gave me, and the twins stood by the door, slowly revolving.

"This is Jane and Jane Rozlapa," I continued. "They're real felons. Murder. They're looking to get to Latvia and you're just the kind of guy who'd be nice enough to give 'em a ride."

"I docked last night," he said. "Haven't seen them, haven't heard from them. Honest."

"I believe you. But you got something on this end. Your flight plan's got you in Moscow next. Riga is on the way. What are you taking to Moscow?"

"Chili," he said smiling.

"As in beef and beans?"

30

"Two tons of the most delectable delicacy. Coming from in from Crooklin, you can check."

"I will."

"So anyway," he went on. "While I have been known to help a jay-walking friend in need, I do not truck with homicide. It's against my scruples."

"Yeah," I said. "But it would be so convenient. I want these girls. You help me and you can keep your sixty-five."

"My sixty-five and two free passes."

"Done."

4 - Jane and the Other Jane

I fined him for improper storage. I had to cover my com-absence so I spun a yarn about needing to look into the ion-pod. Cook got off cheap and my bosses were satisfied with the cash. The nurses gave me a lot of crap, so I got Charlotte and we did an inspection. We found a bunch of wince; a real nasty euphoric. They tried to bribe me but the bust would look good on Charlotte's record, so off they went. Besides, their bribe was laughable. What can I say; the job just begs your little corruptions. The other ships were clean. More or less. It was a fairly profitable day.

I pulled a twelve hour shift, but I cleared my decks. I made sure to call Geena; we had a thing about my being home late from work.

There was nothing scheduled till late that next afternoon so I had the morning off. I slept in. I checked in with Alistair and just left a message. I didn't tell him about Cookie.

I had a late breakfast in the study. I was trying to get something on the Janes. There was nothing on any media. I used my Bureau password to ding into NCIC, but the Feds had nothing on the girls. I checked the Province of Eastern New England. Zip. There was zero in the DOC, provincial or federal. I looked into Boston Unified Police District, civil and criminal. It was like these girls weren't known to anybody. So was Alistair lying to me, or was the hunt that secret? I had no clue as to where to begin looking.

And then they came to me. Literally.

"Incoming," Geena said strolling into the room. "The pool service is at the gate."

"Tell them to take a hike. It's not even April."

She paused. She looked confused. Then she said, "They said to say, 'Jessie Dog'."

"Shit," I muttered. "Let them in."

I watched the monitor as the gate slid open and the ground van pulled in. I went around back to meet it. The driver jumped out dressed in coveralls, sporting a full shock of silver hair and beard. But there was no mistake. I'd know those blue eyes and that gaunt face anywhere.

"Shelly-bird," I gasped.

"Jessica," she said rushing to embrace me. "Jessie-dog I need your help. I really, really need your help."

Shelly was a fellow Uptown survivor. She was tall and slender to the point of emaciation. The fever's stomach bug had a field day with her and did a number on her digestive system. The girl had to eat a lot to stay alive. She had gotten her Friday a while ago, but she had paid for it.

"Shelly-bird what is it? What?"

But even as I spoke the side door to the van opened and two young girls jumped out. They were twins. They were dressed for travel and they looked like they had traveled. They had sailor boots that ran over their calves and tan leather leggings. They were draped in olive drab wool wrap ponchos with high collars and a bunch of zippered pockets that jangled as they jumped out. Their hair still had streaks of blue but it was obvious that they hadn't seen a bottle of dye in a while. Their make-up was still crisp but their eyes seemed haunted.

And they had double eyebrows.

"Jessie," Shelly said, "these are Randy Phelps kids."

"Hi," one said. "I'm Jane,"

"and I'm the other Jane."

"You're twins," I managed.

"No," Jane said rolling her eyes.

"we're faking it," the other Jane said.

"I just love"

"going around"

"and looking like her."

"It's great"

"for getting dates."

It was too weird. They were like mirrors of each other. They talked as one, their facial gestures were harmonized, and when one slung a hip the other did the same only opposite.

"Who's Randy Phelps?" I asked.

"Our dad."

"In a way."

"The genius."

"You had to read about him,"

"and his Sparkle Prize,"

"for genetic engineering."

"More like tinkering."

"And bumbling."

"He died in Oslo."

"Right after the ceremony."

"Got assassinated."

"They say it was the Ruskies."

"They say he pissed 'em off."

34

"That'd be just like him."

"Always pissing people off."

I was taken by the banter. Then I was taken by what they said. Then I looked them over.

"So who did you kill?" I asked.

"Huh?" they said in unison.

I looked at them. Shelly looked at me.

"Jessie-dog, we gotta talk."

"Ya think?"

We sat around the kitchen table. Geena put out a bowl of chips and banana-dip. Shelly peeled off the beard and wig. She was bald as a baby. She scarfed. I snapped on the shield.

"Nice place," Jane said.

"Roomy,"

"and safe."

"We drove up from Providence."

"South Boston was such fun."

"Drive?" I asked.

"Like in a car," Jane said.

"On the road," her sister added.

"Armored."

"Funsville."

"So who'd you kill along the way?" I asked.

"I don't know what you're talking about," they said.

"Jessie?" Shelly asked. "Why do you think that they killed anyone?"

"Anyone plural," I said. "Because that's what I was told. I was told that you two murdered two people and that you're in town to find a way to Latvia."

Even their giggling was harmonic.

"Who told you that?" Shelly asked.

"That's not important," I said, "So what's going on?"

"I don't know anything about any murders," Shelly said. "Or Latvia. We're trying to get these girls to Montana."

"So why all the cloak and dagger?"

"We're wanted," Jane said.

"But not for murder."

"Just for being us."

The two looked at me smiling, batting their eyelashes and dancing their brows.

Shelly explained that they had been one of Randy Phelps' experiments. Almost twenty years ago, after the second Scandinavian war, the place was wasted. Their mother was under government welfare and so her profile popped up on somebody's screen. Along with about a dozen other women she was drafted into the state's genetic research program, sponsored by Randy Phelps.

Long story short, nine months later out came a crop of savants. The kids tested off the charts in everything. That was nothing new. Super-brains were popping out all over the place, even without any modifications. But the two Janes were different. They weren't better than any of the other kids, they weren't smarter, but they were different in that they thought faster. Researchers suspected telepathy, or something on those lines. And so a lot of people were interested.

They were sixteen years old when Riga collapsed. They were smuggled out by one of their

36

nannies and for two years they ran and hid all across Europe until they finally caught up with Amnesty Inter-Colonial who got them on a slow boat to the states. They wanted to get to New York but ended up in New Haven. Shelly was Amnesty's girl in this end.

"So why Montana?" I asked.

"It's in the heart of the Free Western Preserve," Shelly said. "They're off the grid, way off. We figure that there these kids can grow up without somebody wanting to snatch them and pick their brains."

"Literally," Jane said.

"You see Jessie," Shelly said, "these two aren't fully developed. They're really not out of adolescence and their brains are still growing. And the big thing is that they're . . . joined; conjoined mentally, somehow."

"They split us up once," Jane said,

"for two months."

"I almost went nuts."

"I almost went nuts."

"They need each other," Shelly said. "Proximity has something to do with it, but the point is that they need a place to grow and mature in security and ease; a place where they can settle down and, well, quite honestly figure themselves out."

"If anyone can do that," Jane said,

"we can."

"Gives a whole new meaning,"

"to finding ourselves."

"Wait a minute," I said. "If you're from Scandinavia, how come you talk like you were born in Roxbury?"

"We're natural mimes," Jane said in a perfect imitation of Shelly's voice.

"It's a survival skill," the other Jane said imitating me.

That was very weird.

And then all three of them were looking at me. The twins were smiling ever so innocently. Shelly's wrinkled brow was furrowed enough to plant peas. It didn't take a savant to figure out why they were in my kitchen.

"And so," I said slowly. "You want me to smuggle you to Helena."

"Amazing," Jane said.

"Brilliant," her sister echoed.

"Don't get snide with me," I said.

"Jessie, they're teenagers."

"Oh, Jayzeus Nice," I said. "Geena, fix me a Manhattan."

"No," she said. "You have to go to work soon."

"Call me in sick."

"No."

"Jessie?" Shelly said.

"I have to think about it."

"Jessie? What's to think about? These girls need your help, and I am asking."

"Michelle, it's complicated," I said, snapping at her. She actually looked hurt. "Shelly you don't understand. This is a real Rudy Meyers."

"Okay," she said after a moment. "Okay. But look, just . . . well if you can't help at least let them

38

stay here a few days until I can figure something out. Jessie? Please?"

I had helped her with some wanted refugees before. Alistair never cared. But these girls were on his radar, and by association mine. And possibly my Friday. But I loved Shelly like a sister. We'd gone through some real hairy shit together. Of course it was like that for all us survivors; a fellow asked you a favor you did it. That was all.

So this was a real mess for me.

Shelly was a do-gooder, a real mother-hen; always had been. She was a volunteer nurse in Uptown Town. She volunteered to go into that anarchic mess. When she made it out alive she took her Friday by giving up her ovaries. She reasoned that that way she'd have a thousand babies. But what she never talked about, and what we never spoke about, was that her eggs would most likely go to slave Farms. Now she was using those motherly instincts working with Amnesty. The way she looked at those two little snots near broke my heart.

I looked to Geena. Her face was impassive. I never knew for sure if she understood the calls she channeled. I don't know why I thought that she could help.

"Mistress," Geena said, "shall I make up the guest room?"

"Yeah."

The twins were overjoyed. They got to sleep on their first real bed in months. But not before Shelly had them bring in their belongings, what they were. Shelly had to return the pool van. The drone eyes would think it weird if it stayed overnight. I went

39

with her in my armor and a sidearm. She needed to take public transit back to the walls of Chelsea and I wasn't going to let her go it alone. We cuddled on the ground bus like lovers. Creeps looked, but no one touched. And the whole ride back I knew that she wanted to ask, but she didn't.

Work was boring that next afternoon. I had two ships and I was in a foul mood. I gave 'em a pass. I was ready to head home when I had a thought. I dinked Interpol and looked up the name Rozlapa and I got five hits, two were named Jane. The Finns and Russians had pics. They were younger, maybe twelve or so, but it was them. I couldn't think why we didn't have them in the states.

I tried to dink Amnesty Inter-Colonial, but they had better security than the Pentagon. At least part of Shelly's story checked out. I scanned the Boston PD Look-Out again, and saw that I was still at large and priority one: the other me. The one with the purple hair and half her head shaved. I knew that they would not stop looking for me. Ever. I tried not to think about that. Maybe Alistair –

But if Alistair ever had a whiff of an idea that I had helped the twins get to the Western Preserve I was dead. Or at least spreading my legs till I died. Life's a funny thing.

It got funnier on the shuttle platform. There I saw Detective-Sergeant Adolpho in all his bald glory. He was chatting to Elijah, one of my supervisors. They were laughing. Elijah saw me and called me over. He introduced me as one of his crack agents. He explained how the Detective was hot to catch a cop killer and how he wanted to be certain that we'd be on the lookout for the woman. Adolpho described Jessica, badly.

"Of course," the ugly said, "she'd be made over, so you nab any people being smuggled be sure to forward the retinas to me. Personally."

"You got it," I said. "We haven't had any bodies trying to exit here in a while. The inspectors will be eager. They'll be real thorough. They're tired of Nasties all the time."

Adolpho chuckled. Then he eyed me strangely. My blood slushed to ice as I tried to remember if I had my blue contacts on.

"You know," he said. "You sound like her."

"I sound like her?"

"Yeah. I'm an old opera buff. I got an ear for voices."

I laughed.

"You have off last weekend?" he asked.

"I did."

"Where were ya?"

"Detective," Elijah put in. "I don't understand—"

"Humor me," he said chuckling. "It's this cop thing. Play along, just for giggles."

"I was home," I shrugged. "With my slave, Geena. You want my retina?"

"No," he said still chuckling. "I want your wrist."

"Beg pardon?"

"Your wrist. Lemme see your wrist. Either one'll do."

41

I had my gloves off and my armor was powered low. I slipped up a sleeve.

"That looks like a cuff mark," he said.

"It is," I said in a sultry voice. "My slave can be a very harsh Mistress."

The two burst out laughing. I saw the scar on ugly's tongue.

"You can ask her," I added.

"Now why would I wanna do that," he said. "She's your slave; she'd say anything you told her to. But who's gonna ask anybody anything? Like I say, it's just this cop thing I got, always asking questions. So anyway, Ms. Teasdale, the bus is here."

"Who's Teasdale?" I asked.

"There I go again. Thank for all your help, Elijah. Time to board, Ms. Waters."

I was saved by Charlotte. She snagged me and we sat together. She talked the whole time about her debriefing on the Nurses bust.

5 - Rudy Meyers

"What's a Rudy Meyers?" Geena asked.

We were snuggling in bed. It wasn't that late but the twins took over the TV. That was fine with me. Shelly had taken to my study. She was hooked with her Amnesty friends looking for another way. Geena had relieved my stress.

"Rudy Meyers was a nut-job back in Uptown Town," I said. "He was on the maintenance crew, but he was crazy even before he caught the fever. He was one of those Earth-First types; loved his guns and his flags. Anyway he took a whole ward hostage. He was demanding to be taken to a real hospital in Chi-town or London. Said he'd kill 'em all. There were more than twenty people on the ward."

"They all had the fever?" she asked.

"Yeah. Late stages. They were all going to die but . . . But anyway he had this tank of cyanogens gas and he'd rigged a dead-man switch. If we zapped him, the room would flood. If we rushed him, the room would flood. If we did nothing the room would flood, and there was no negotiating with the asshole. So this was before Shelly and I had got infected. I was . . . in security and it was her ward. It was an impossible situation."

"So what happened?"

"Shelly wanted to rush him. I told her if the guy saw hazy-suits they'd all be dead before she touched the doorknob. She wanted to go it alone, no suit, right then and there. That's the way she is. She thinks that if there a chance she has to take it. I couldn't talk her out of it, so I clobbered her and zapped Rudy. Everybody died."

"It was," Geena said. "An impossible situation."

"Hence the name; Rudy Meyers. Shelly hated me for a while after that. But, well in a situation like that you get over things. Other shit happens."

"Poor dear."

"So anyway," I said. "How'd you get on with tweedle-twins."

"They slept for a long time," she said. "Then I fed them. They were astonished at our fridge and went gaga over eggs. I made them breakfast."

I had to chuckle at that. She slapped my ass.

"Anyway," she went on. "They got snooty; challenged me to a game of Knights and Queens."

"How did that go?"

"They're brilliant. And cocky. I wiped the board with them."

"That musta got 'em."

"They actually accused me of cheating," she said in a huff. "So I replayed the game move by move and pointed out where they went wrong. By the end of our second game they were asking me questions and picking my brain about strategy. By supper we were friends. But, um mistress?"

"Yeah?"

"We spent some time in the laundry. They really don't have much. I had to give them some underwear. I'd like to use some of the house money to get them some things. If that's okay."

"Use my money," I said, "And replace your underwear."

44

"Thank you mistress," she said kissing me.

"And as long as your shopping," I said thinking. "I'd like you to buy some handcuffs and, um things."

"Handcuffs and things, mistress?"

"Let me explain, Mistress . . ."

Despite Geena's tender care I couldn't sleep. I put on a robe and went up to my tower pad. I loved looking over the city at night. I loved the way the rivers drew boundaries between the lights of the different sections. The fires cast a soft sort of glow while the twinkling night-life sparkled like stars. The traffic lanes above ran smooth in the night, and they always made me think of blood arteries and veins; the white-blue rushing oxygen in as the red sped toxins out. Up above a gibbous moon was bright through the haze and I could see Neilstown glowing purple on the shadow side.

"It's a nice view," Shelly said.

She startled me. I didn't see her.

"I followed you up," she said. "Hope you don't mind?"

"No," I said. "I'm glad for your company. So, you got any leads?"

"There's a fellow in Youngstown who is willing to help."

"Youngstown is like five, maybe six hundred miles."

Shelly shrugged.

"How you gonna get there?"

"There's a network of ground cars," she said. "They're expensive but Amnesty trusts them."

"You'll never get through Springfield," I said.

"Jessie, those two girls got across Europe to Lisbon. I think they'll get through that silly zone."

"Then there's Pennslytucky."

"Jessie, why can't you help?"

I shut my eyes.

"Jessie, if it's money—"

"It ain't money!" I said turning and glaring at her. "How could you think such a thing?"

"Because it's the only thing I have," she said. "And I am so used to dealing with people who will help for a price. I'm sorry. It's what I work with and it's all that I have—that and our friendship."

"It's Alistair," I blurted.

"Holy shit."

"There ain't nothing holy about this shit," I said.

"Jessie? Alistair?"

"I sold out. Okay?"

"No," she said. "It's not okay, because you didn't sell out. He's got your Friday, doesn't he?"

I wanted to cry. I wanted to cry like a little girl and fall into Shelly's arms and tell her everything. I wanted to tell her about all of the things that he made me do; I wanted to tell her about all of the sordid encounters I had just to get a dose of angel tears. I wanted to tell her that I just wanted to stay alive. I didn't care about money or Samantha's fancy house or any of that shit. I had been through hell and back and now I just wanted to stay alive.

But I didn't do that. I opened my eyes and looked out over the colors of light cut by the rivers.

"I," I began, "I do things for him. Security things. Black ops. The twins are on my plate. He

46

wants them. He was the one who told me about the murders and Riga and all that bullshit. He lied. But he still has my Friday, and, Shelly-bird, you know how that is. But you know me. You know I'd never turn them over. But if he ever even suspected that I helped –"

"Jessie?"

"What?"

"How do you know that he's not lying about Friday?"

"What?"

"How do you know—"

"I heard you."

I had thought about that one. The Friday wasn't generic. It was a scaffold and it had to be tailored specific. Alistair had my brain scans and all my profiles. He was there in Uptown Town. He was the one, in those last dark and dirty days, who wouldn't let us die. We were goners, and while the other wards would do their best to make their patients comfortable, Alistair would keep pumping us with fluids and nutrients because –"Because you want to stay alive," he'd say.

And we believed him. And we survived. And he got so much smarter.

"He's my only hope," I said. "If he's lying, I am dead."

"That may not be true," Shelly said. "He may not be your only hope."

"He was there. He's got all the data. He's got the power, and he's got my salvation."

"And you got two savants who need your help."

"What are you saying?"

"I'm saying that these girls can be your other hope," Shelly said. "You could go with. You could give them time. They might be able to come up with something for you. I know they'd love the challenge."

"And in the mean time?" I said. "While I wait for them to mature and so come up with something?"

"There's touch heads in the Preserve," she said. "There's touch heads everywhere. You could live. Right now you're waiting for Alistair and believing his word. I promise you that my girl's word would be a real. And they wouldn't dangle it. They'd chase it."

Rudy Meyers again and again. I had only Shelly's notion that the twins would do what she said. Meantime I had Alistair. Both ideas had the promise of more time and more bullshit. It was like both of them had my dead-man switch.

I had always prided myself on being decisive. So why couldn't I decide?

"You need to sleep," Shelly said.

"No," I said. "I need clarity. Let's go talk with Jane and Jane."

"Absolutely."

They were asleep. Shelly warned me to be careful. I opened the door slowly, but that wasn't careful enough. In a flash they were out of bed, on either side of the room and laser beams were on our foreheads.

"Wakie-wakie," Shelly sang.

The beams snapped off and the lights snapped on.

"What's up?" they said calm as calm.

They stashed their pistols, sat on the bed and we had a nice long talk.

6 - Persuasions

I knew my first move and I knew that I had to work fast.

The next morning at work I had two little ships and a slow boat from Barcelona. One of the littles was squeaky clean, so I flagged it. Anybody that clean was moving nasties. I really don't care much what people want to sneak into my city, but I draw the line with euphorics; me and my scruples. The slow boat took all flipping morning.

I had lunch in my office; pastrami from *Nathan's*. I figured I wasn't long for this world so I splurged. I called my buddy Rashid from Chemistry. His smiling brown face was always such a pleasure to see.

"Hey there, Happy," I said. "How's Honey?"

"Sammie," he said looking glad to see me. "She is so fine. So glad she is mine. And I have – whoa, what's this?"

I shot him my scan from the May Queen. He was the pro and I watched his eyes looking intently.

"Somebody ripped a good one," he said chuckling. Then he started, "Female, adult, healthy, usual stuff, nothing jumps out at me. What do you need?"

"This is from a little ship I want to flag," I said. "Something, I don't know. You know how sometimes you just get a hunch? Anyway I want to hold the crew. Can you give me anything?"

"Well," he said pondering. "There's a trace – and I do mean a trace of Dengue. But a good lawyer could get that tossed quick."

"They won't have time. So that means I can quarantine them?"

"You could . . . oh wait, here's something. Opioid. Probably from a poppy seed bun."

"Mmmm, lemon. Love 'em," I said, smiling

"So you'll need my stamp on this."

"You know," I said. "I just got me a bottle of eighty-proof Vesta whiskey."

"Sammie, I'm Muslim."

"But your boss isn't," I said grinning. "And it's his birthday tomorrow."

He laughed. That flipping bureaucracy killed me. Amazing anything ever got done. So we chatted while I set up my warrant. He stamped it and that was that. Cookie's crew would have a rough twenty-four hours up at the station, but they were used to that sort of thing.

It took the good captain less than ninety minutes to come storming into my office. He had actually found my office in that bee-hive. I liked that. Showed determination. He was dressed in his flight suit. Looked like I had stepped on a plan.

"What the flup are you doing?" he demanded.

"Captain," I said. "Watch your language."

"You snagged my crew."

"If you bothered to read the warrant—"

"We had a poppy-seed cake," he said. "If you check the kitchen—"

"We will."

51

"And nobody's got Dengue," he said fuming. "And even if they did why the hell would you care? Nobody's coming downside and I got an appointment in Moscow."

"Hey, some of my best friends are Ruskies."

"You son of a bitch, I thought that we had a—"

"Captain!" I cried slamming the desk. "Watch your language around here. This ain't some dockside tavern."

I glared at him and raised an eyebrow. With one finger I toyed with my hair while using my pinky to point to the lens on my suit. I was in armor. His teeth clenched, but he got me.

"I'm sorry," he said. "Just a little stressed. So look, I want to be cooperative, so I just thought that you might help me help my crew. Is there anything that I can do?"

"You could take me to dinner," I said, chuckling.

He just looked at me.

"Just let things play out," I said. I stood and got my things. "In twenty-four you'll be on your way to the mother-land and your chili will be none the worse. Now it's been a long day and I just want to go home. Sure you don't want to take me out to dinner?"

I showed him my phone. My address was blazing. I slowly shook my head.

"N-next time I'm in port," he said.

"Too bad. If you change your mind I'm usually home by seven."

"Sorry, I'm real busy."

The bus was delayed. We sat idling on the platform waiting and there were no announcements. I just wanted to get home, I was dog tired. I had gotten little sleep the night before so I leaned against the window and tried to doze. I wondered if I should call Geena. After a while there was a commotion. My eyes fluttered open and my heart stopped. There was a flyer parked beside us with blue gumballs flashing on top. I heard boots up the gangway.

"Agent Waters," somebody called out. "Agent Samantha Waters."

I looked. There were four cops, two women and two men. They had their weapons out. They found me. They checked my ID, then they grinned.

"Sergeant Adolpho would like to have a word with you," one of them said.

"Doesn't he have my number?"

"Oh he's got your number alright. Let's go."

They had needle guns. That was a sort of a good sign. They wanted me alive and if I put up a fuss it would be sleepy-bye. But that was also a sort of a bad sign. They wanted me alive. My suit would have withstood their darts, but in the close quarters of the bus they had a clean shot at my neck. I figured that I stood a better chance outside.

"Okie-dokie," I said holding up my palms.

In the aisle they flanked me, two in front and two behind. They took my purse.

"Ms. Waters," one of the women said. "Your armor."

"What about it?"

"It's procedure," she said. "I have to ask you to remove it."

"What?"

"We'll help you if you need."

"Um, is there, like somewhere we can go?"

"M'am, please remove your suit."

"Here?"

The two women slung their weapons. They were big. Before they could, I started unzipping. Every eye on the bus was on me, and a lot of heads were craning. I must have flushed three shades of red. In a moment I was standing there in nothing but a pair of yellow lace panties and a pair of nickel plated handcuffs. They took my suit. They led me away. I was mortified.

But even as we walked I realized that something wasn't right. They'd cuffed me wrong; my palms were together. That's when I started getting real afraid. People were still staring at me through the bus windows as the four led me to the car. The tarmac was freezing on my bare feet.

When we got to the car I knew that something was way off. The women took the front seats and the men ushered me into the back. Nobody protected my head. The back of the car was like nothing I'd ever seen. It was deep. There was a bench seat at the far end, but there was also a single straight-back seat facing rear. I was slammed into that. There was a hollow behind for my arms. Straps went around my legs and thighs forcing me spread open. More straps went around my belly and then above and below my breasts. The car took off.

I just grinned and shook my head.

"You're not real cops," I said chuckling, as the car rose

The men grinned back. They tore off my wig and then they started placing electrodes on my body in the most intimate places.

"This is gonna hurt," I said. "Isn't it?"

Fire raced through me in reply. My body jerked and thrashed straining against the bonds. I flung back my head but no sound came out. Then just as fast as it started it disappeared and I collapsed in the chair. I groaned.

"Where are they," one of them asked.

"Where are whoo—nnggg --"

Liquid lightning charged through damn near every fiber of my being. It was like they had poured lava through my veins, and it went on and on. When it finally stopped I had nearly cut myself pulling at the straps and I was awash in sweat. The two were gazing at me with lustful grins.

"Martha," I managed. "My friend Martha has them."

"Where is Martha?"

"I don't--"

The searing pain had doubled again and I writhed in its agony. My body was jolting and jerking. The cops were speaking but I could hear nothing beyond my own shrieks. I burst into tears and was still screaming and begging long after the pain ceased.

We went back and forth like that. By the fifth jolt I thought that I'd twist my spine out of place. I was actually crying, begging them to believe me. My wrists were bleeding.

"Listen to me you stupid bitch," one of the cops said digging his nails into my nipple. "You're dead. That's all. The only question is how you're going to die. You take us to the girls and you get a tap in the back of your head and that's that. You give us any more shit and we dump you on Adolpho's doorstep."

"After we've had a time with your sorry ass," the other said. "Cutie."

"Are those girls that important to you?" the first asked.

Still weeping I gave them my address. The car wheeled. We had been over the water all that time.

"Who's going to be there?"

Before I could answer I got another quick jolt. Pain.

"The twins," I said gasping. "They're sick. They've been bedridden since . . . since they came to me. And . . . and Martha . . . hnnnnnnggg!"

"Who else?"

"Maybe . . . maybe Leon . . . he's, he's with Amnesty. He's making the arrangements."

"Doing good cutie. Now what about security at the house?"

I gave up everything. Then I begged and begged them not to kill me, promising all sorts of wild things. If they were pros they weren't very experienced. They should have put me on hold somewhere while someone went to case the place. But they seemed in a hurry. I just prayed that Geena was on the ball.

They landed at my house in silent mode. All four got out. They dragged me from the car and held my eye over the lock. The latch clicked open and they shoved me into the dark foyer. When nothing happened they all burst in shouting "Police!"

They had the moves down as they fanned. There was a squeal from the parlor. Two burst in with weapons pointed while two covered them from the hall. Geena screamed.

"What the flup?" a cop said, half chuckling.

In the firelight Geena and some guy were half naked and wrestling. Geena looked up and squealed.

Then there were two loud pops and the cops on guard outside the room were pasted against the wall. Geena launched. She did an aerial flip and her heels caught the other two square in their faces. I heard crunching and they crumbled. But armor had protected the two outside and the bullets had simply punched them. They recovered fast.

"Drop it!" a voice cried from the shadows.

"Or you're dead!" came the echo.

I saw the lasers bobbing on the wall beside their foreheads. Then there were two simultaneous flashes from above me, and the wall by the heads of the two cops erupted. One of them started firing blindly. His face exploded. The other one dropped her pistol and raised her hands. The twins dropped from the ceiling. One held her gun to the cop's head while the other took position by the front door.

"That's all of them," I said.

"We're clear in here," Geena called from the parlor.

The lights snapped on. I got to my feet. I looked over and saw Cookie with a gun pointing at a cop on the floor.

57

"Um," he said to me, "you're not dressed."
I got dressed.

Geena and I had a thing. If I was going to be late I'd call. If I didn't call there was trouble. She's such a smart girl. Cookie had taken me up on my dinner invite, and Geena and Shelly knew that I was looking at him as a way out. When they saw the car landing Geena worked up that surprise. She figured that her boobs would throw them off just enough. How the Janes had suspended themselves from the foyer ceiling we could never figure.

"Just something,"

"that we do," they shrugged.

Shelly had stayed hidden the whole time. There was not much she could do.

Two of the cops were dead; one had his face blown off and the other had his nose bone in his brain. The others clammed up, but when I offered to take them for a ride in their own car the woman sang so sweetly.

They were from the Phelps Institute. They wanted their babies back. Those corporate heavies were usually military rejects who thought themselves something. They had all of the toys and none of the experience. The Janes and Cookie had them trussed up good in a closet, after relieving them of their armor and toys.

Geena saw to my boo-boos. I wanted to learn more from the two goons and I was looking so forward to that. But first it was time to sit down with Cookie.

58

The Janes were playing with the cop's armor and toys while Shelly and I sat at the kitchen table and explained things to Cookie. Geena served very stiff Manhattans. I offered Cookie my sixty-five bounty on the girls, and Geena tossed in the money she'd have spent on a land crossing.

"It's a straightforward job," he said. "Lord knows I done enough of 'em. But what bothers me is why the hell you had to use my crew."

"I needed to keep you in port," I said. "I needed to get your attention and I needed you to come to me. I can get you clearances and you can be in Moscow tonight. Then a short trip to Montana and you're on your way back to Up-base Nine, then home to Vesta in the morning."

"Simple like that."

"Yeah."

"Nothing's ever simple."

Shelly looked at him so pleadingly.

"Okay," he said. "Here's the deal. I'll take your money and I'll do a side trip to Montana. But I still got those two passengers you so cleverly discovered still stashed on board the *May Queen* and I suspect that they're getting uncomfortable. I got the drop worked out. There's this fellow has a boat; goes fishing off the Georges Banks. It's well beyond the twelve mile limit. I meet him there in the lander, I make the drop, I bundle up your Janes, and we go our ways. Now, I'm gonna be asking my boatman to take two passengers out to that meet—"

"Three," I said. "I'm going with."

"Three," he nodded. "So he's gonna want something for that."

"I can cover that," I said.

"And he may need some convincing."

"I got that too," I said.

"Okay. Now he's got his boat down at Jeffries Point."

"You're for shit," I said. "You want me to take those two young girls through that neighborhood?"

"From what I seen, those two young girls can handle themselves."

"I can help you mistress," Geena said softly.

My heart sank. In all of my scheming I hadn't factored in Geena. Somewhere in the back of my mind I had thought that I'd give her to Shelly. She's be good working with Amnesty. But now that it came to it I realized that it wouldn't be that simple for me. I just nodded and said a soft "thank you".

"Well alrighty then," Cookie said. "Let's see to some details."

In my study I got him the clearances for his ship and his lander. Shelly transferred her money. Then he and I argued about his crew. He wanted them released immediately. Even if that were possible I wouldn't do it. I hardly knew this guy and they were my ace in the hole.

"You'll get them back," I said. "When the twins and I are safe."

He ranted and I threatened to hold them another twenty-four. He shut up. I knew he was pissed, but I also knew that he had a certain respect for my balls. All that was left was to plot a timetable. Cookie got on to his man with the boat. Just then the Janes came racing up the stairs.

"Tante Geena,"

"Tante Shelly,"
"according to the radios"
"on these suits"
"company's coming"
"and they sound like policemen!"
"Real policemen!"
"Tell me you got a plan," Cookie said.

7 - Evasion

"Everybody in the parlor," I said calmly. "Now."

Geena knew what to do. From my monitor I saw that the cops were seventy seconds away. They had lights flashing but sirens quiet.

I typed in a code. In less than twenty seconds my garage opened and my car lifted. Thirteen seconds later it sped out due west in a line and altitude that ignored traffic lanes. I saw two patrol cars peel away as I grabbed my kit. I made it to the parlor even as the others cars were landing. Geena had the rug up and the door opened. I dashed down the stairs with the others, and she sealed us in and replaced the rug and coffee table.

The moment the hatch shut all sound from upstairs was cut off. We were safe but it would be two minutes before I knew if Geena was.

"What the heck," everybody said in a sort of unison -- but not all with the same words.

The land under Chelsea is sandy; hard to build basements. Not impossible but expensive. Most people built on slabs. But this place was built in the height of what was known as the Cold War. It was a time when people thought that they could shelter against nukes; such a quaint notion. But thinking that notion, the original builders had constructed a pretty little bomb shelter under their parlor. People had big families back then so the place was roomy. The reinforced concrete was a good shield against penetrating radar, not that cops used that, but it was a comfort.

Somewhere along the house's history, in happier times, someone had turned the shelter into a sound recording studio. It was ear-proof. Samantha had brought it up to speed as a panic room. Geena and I made some finishing touches. The place was comfy and safe.

"What about Tante Geena?" Jane cried.

"Where is she!" the other yelled.

I waved them away. I had to drive.

I dashed to the consol. It felt like it took forever before my car cams activated. The scene was frightening at first. The car was on auto and darting and dodging as it crossed the One-North Sky-lane. I flinched as it skirted a commuter bus. In a moment it broke the lane and I saw the Bennington Groundway glowing below, and open water beyond. I took the controls. Something sparkled off the port quarter panel. The cops were shooting. I really didn't want any civilians hurt, but those jerks didn't care if they dropped the thing on the middle of Winthrop. Jackasses.

I punched it and started zigzagging. The engine red lined. It just needed it to hold together a few minutes more. A stabilizer started to shudder so I eased back on the evasion. More sparks came from starboard and above. The Coast Guard was there. They could use snag lines. If they did, that would shred the car, and I couldn't have a wreck. I needed annihilation. I dove. I could almost hear the turbo screaming. Then I saw black – the beautiful black of water below.

I was clear of any innocents. I breathed.

I lost that stabilizer and the car started to careen. The shooting stopped and the car was bathed in white light. I watched the altimeter. At twenty feet above sea level I hit the go button. Then the screen went fuzzy, then cut out.

If I timed it right the explosion would have happened just as the thing hit the water. If I didn't it was no big deal. There were enough heavy explosives in the frame to keep them searching for weeks.

I collapsed in the chair.

"What about Geena!"

"Checking now," I said. I took up my phone and said softly, "Santa?"

"Ho ho ho," came the softer reply.

She switched off but I kept mine on.

"She's cool," I said. "Well, not exactly."

The plan was actually Alistair's. He'd invested a lot in me and wanted to keep me safe, the sweetheart. Any baddies looking for me in my own home would be savvy enough to figure there'd be a safe room. And they'd look in the usual spots. No one would think to look under a rug on a house built on a slab, unless that rug was all mussed up.

"So Geena," Jane said, working it out. "Fixes the rug."

"Complete with coffee table," I added.

"And then?"

"Up the chimney she goes," I said.

"What?" Jane gasped.

"There's a fire," her sister cried.

"in the fireplace."

"She's a slave," I reminded them. "She can take it. Well, for a little while anyway. But she's got a shield up there and a breathy thingie."

"Jayzeus"

"Nice."

"How long can she hold out?" Shelly asked.

"Two hours," I said. "Then she's got options. She can bank the fire. If there's no sky-eyes she can crawl out and go to another hidey-hole. Or she can shut down."

"What about us?" Cookie asked.

"Two weeks," I said. "Just, go easy on the TP."

"And that whole car thing," Cookie mulled. "That was quite the diversion. If they think that you lit out and died then they'll not be too thorough in your house. Just the usual ruin. Very smart. Very frosty. It's just that I see that as a very expensive rig, but never mind. So what's going on upstairs? You got cams?"

"Yeah," I said "But I don't like the idea of running them while they're snooping. I'm gonna give them a few hours."

"Fantastic. Now all we need is a deck of cards."

I didn't have a deck of cards. The twins amused themselves with my food stores. Shelly joined them and I didn't care. We weren't under siege and I knew that I'd never see this house again. Besides the kids hadn't seen this much variety since who could say.

I pulled Shelly aside. I broached the idea about giving her Geena. As I figured, the activist in her wrankled. I started to get a lecture on Cyborg rights, and I rolled my eyes. Sometimes bleeding hearts could get way out of hand.

I mean, I was okay with the Cetacean Bill of Rights and all. They were mammals and they had brains and language and societies, and if they had hands they might actually accomplish something. So that was cool. But when people started pushing for ant colonies and beehives I thought that over the edge.

Slaves were another thing entirely. They had no innate drive for anything other than survival. There was that weird movement a few years back where people started buying them up and burning their papers, thinking that they were setting the slaves free. All those liberated cyborgs did was eat, sleep, piss and shit. They didn't even have a sex drive. Without direction they were like a computer without an operator. Very powerful, but couldn't do much other than keep time.

And the whole artificial intelligence thing turned out to be vapor. At the heart of any thinking machine was the core of a thought instilled by the creator, and so really all it did was follow that core to the safest, easiest and most logical conclusions. Those conclusions didn't lead to world domination or human extinction. They were too logical for that.

Of course the other end of AI was a dud too. Those who gave the super-machines the germ of saving humanity were served up all sorts of social and political solutions like the equal distribution of wealth, free education, housing and health care. That went nowhere fast.

But if you gave a normal, thinking and autonomous machine like Geena a task or a goal, you gave them a purpose and they ran with that and they learned.

Sometimes.

Geena was a fabulous lover and a rotten cook, but both tasks made her happy. Isn't that what it's all about in the end?

"Happiness?" Shelly asked me.

"Yeah," I said. "What else do we have in this veil of tears?"

"Fulfillment."

"Geena can climax."

Shelly just looked at me. Sometimes I really didn't get her.

"So look," she said, finally. "If you want her to go with me I'll take her. I'll figure out something."

"You know that you don't have to tell your bosses," I said. "She's really good at passing. One time I got her into—"

"I'll figure something out."

"Cool."

She just nodded a kind of sad looking nod.

The time dragged. I so wanted to look through my spy cams but I knew that it hadn't been that much time. The twins were playing roach-a-bow with Cookie and feasting on Nollyoaty bars. I sat in a lounger and let my brain relax. But the aroma of those treats invaded. I was just about go and grab one when my phone toned.

"ho ho."

"Shut the lights," I said. "We're clear."

A moment later the door opened and the stairs unfolded.

"Merry Chrisptmiss," Geena said.

We emerged to a very dimly lit parlor. It was dark outside. The room was in shambles.

"Keep it low," Geena said. "They got ears outside. And stay away from the windows. The neighbors are peeping."

"You oksy?" I asked.

"I am."

She might have been okay, but she was a mess. She was covered in soot from her head to her foot, and there were places on her boots, her ass and her hair that were singed. She smelled of creosote.

"Tante Geena," the Janes gasped in their whispers.

"I'm ok, girls," she said. "Mistress, the place is a crime scene. They barred the doors and windows and they got a perimeter."

I looked to the parlor picture window. It shimmered so prettily with their lock-downs. Outside the sea mist would sparkle now and then in their laser net.

"They even capped the chimney," Geena said.

"What does that mean?" Shelly asked. "Are we trapped?"

"No," Geena and I said, sounding like the twins in harmony.

"We got a bolt hole," I said. "Cookie, how did you get here?"

"I rented a car," he said. "I thought we were going to dinner."

I slumped against the wall in blessed relief.

"Where is it?"

"I don't know," he said "It landed and I parked it. It's up in some lot somewhere."

"I need to know where it is," I said. "Did you get a code or a card?"

"I went cheap."

"Lors bless you," I said. "May I have that card please?"

He handed it to me. I handed it to Geena. She ran her ring-finger nail across the thin plastic strip, closed her eyes and a moment later smiled.

"Okay," I said. "We gotta go."

"But," Jane said.

"our clothes"

"our new clothes"

"that Tante Geena'

"bought us"

"just for us."

The only hurry was Cookie's. The cop's bars weren't going anywhere. Cookie shrugged.

Their room was strewn. So was every room in the place and the two fake cops were gone. The twins rummaged through the ruins like weasels. They found underwear and tops, bottoms and socks. I changed into my spare armor. The twins greedily stuffed their treasures into their rucksacks.

"Okay?" I asked. "You guys good to go now?"

"What are these?" Jane said rooting through a silk satin bag.

Geena grabbed it. I heard the handcuffs and things clink. And I could have sworn that I saw Geena blush.

"They are not yours," she said. "Now we must go."

I really wanted to grab some precious bits, but that wasn't going to be. The two girls fell in line and we marched back down to the parlor, then to the shelter. Geena closed and locked the door behind. Then she welded the locks with her sonic pen. I took out our Go-Packs from the locker, took out the pistol, checked it and tossed Geena her pack. I stood before the refrigerator and aimed.

"Mistress," Geena said threading her hands with mine. "Allow me to assist. Cartridges are suddenly at a premium."

"Okay," I said. "It's your aero-plane."

She guided my aim and together we pulled off seven shots. The bolts we hit burped and burst, then the fridge hefted and settled. The air smelled acrid. All for one we grabbed the big box and pulled it from the wall. The hole beyond was black and the air smelled stale.

"What is this?" Shelly said.

"Our bolt hole," I said.

I jumped in. I landed on crunchy dark dirt. I turned on my helmet light. The walls were round but it was level beneath my feet. Small clouds of dust burst up from my boots, and then settled. There was a weird smell of stale air and something I didn't want to think about.

The twins leapt in next kicking up a bunch of the dust. Shelly came in scolding them, her light glowing wildly about. Then Cookie dropped in. He stood still and scanned his light.

70

"Now what do we have here?" he said with a small chuckle.

"It's a last resort," I said. "We go this way."

"No wait a minute," Jane said

"There's something like a plaque or medallion here," the other added.

"We got to go," I said.

"No wait."

"There's something here."

"This could be a find."

"This is no find," I said. "We need to go."

"You hear about things like this," Jane said.

"all the time."

"Somebody looks in grandma's basement"

"and whammo – they're thousandaires."

"Jane and Jane," I said. "This ain't grandma's basement."

"There's letters here,"

"GBSD."

"And a number."

"Number forty-nine."

"So that means"

"there are forty-eight others."

"And all like this one!"

"And all full of—"

"Shit," Geena said.

My slave stood holding her light to the two girls.

"Greater Boston Sewage District," she said. "Tunnel number forty-nine. You are standing in grandma's petrified poop. Wanna check out the other forty-eight tunnels?"

8 - Flight

Geena led the way. We plod on for almost an hour, turning here and there into different tunnels and byways. We left a most excellent trail, were anyone following us. We finally had to get onto hands and knees. Geena assured us that we had left the sewer and that were in an old storm drain. I can't remember the last time we had a storm. Dry leaves crunched beneath us.

The first time that we saw light streaming down from above everybody got all excited. But Geena just shook her head and we kept going. Twelve grates later she smiled. Above us there was a narrow downspout about twenty-four inches around and a good twelve feet up. There were no handholds. We heard weird roaring noises from above sounding like distant dragons.

"What is that?" I asked.

"Don't know," Geena said with a frown. "But this is where we need to be."

She dropped her pack and said, "Wait here."

Like we had a choice?

Geena stared up a few seconds, took a few deep breaths and jumped. She launched in a line straight to the grating. Just before she hit it her hands and feet slammed the tube and she held herself there a moment. Then, stayed only by her feet she let go with her hands and her fingers probed above and behind her head. She found a hold. Once stable her legs dangled. Then in a move worthy of a contortionist she curled her legs and then flung them up, her boots slamming the grate. There was a small clang, but that was all. She dangled, took another few breaths and slammed it again. This time the grate lifted a smidge. Her third try popped the thing almost an inch. Then she dropped down, flexing her fingers and grimacing.

"Shit," she breathed.

"I can do that," Jane said.

"So can I," the other Jane added.

They doffed their packs and leapt. They landed on either side of each other gripping opposite ends of the ledge as Geena had. Then, without a word they started to swing and kick. Their combined effort had the grate up and askew within five tries.

"Girls got potential," Geena said.

The three made a human chain and in no time we were all up and out. I was the last, and when I got to the surface I didn't quite understand what I was seeing.

We were at the edge of a paved area. There were a lot of eerie, yellowy lights, but they were all so low. A little ahead of us I saw a line of ground cars like I'd never see in my life. They were all gleaming in brilliant colors; yellows and reds and green and blues. They all had their hoods up and their engines were growling. Every now and then there was a throaty roar. People were walking about like it was some kind of carnival, munching, talking and looking at the cars. Some were dressed real weird in crazy antique leather jackets and stuff.

"We in the right place?" I asked.

"Yeah," Geena said. "This is the Mystic Market. The captain's car park is straight above."

"Let's go see!" the Janes cried with glee.

But even as they started to run Shelly had them by their tall collars.

"Let's walk this way," she said. "And I mean walk."

We skirted the line of cars. We looked a sight. We were dusty and filthy from our underground trek, and Geena hadn't gotten all the soot off her face. But nobody took any notice of a band of raggadies. Off to our left was saw people lining Second Street, cheering and waving as cars raced down the old strip. 'Insane', I thought. To our right there were dozens of vendors selling machine parts and beer. We finally saw a poster announcing the *American Muscle Car Club of Massachusetts*. They were antique buffs.

"People spend money on this stuff?" Cookie said looking around and chuckling.

"Good money," I said. "You see the price of beer?"

"What's beer?" the Janes asked.

"*Alus*," Shelly answered.

"Ohhh! Can we—"

"No."

We had a small shock when we saw flashing police lights, but that too was a showpiece. The warbling siren it wailed was very annoying. We asked around and finally found the car drop. We had to pay fifteen slivers each to access. Cookie waved his card and inside of five minutes his rental hovered before us. It was a cheap saucer, but it was roomy.

74

"You were going to take me to dinner in this?" I asked.

"What?" he said. "Too good for you?"

Once we were all safely tucked inside I felt a wave of relief flood over all of us. We all took the time to breathe.

The plan was for Cookie to fly us south to the waterfront. Rentals had governors that kept them out of certain sections of the city, so he couldn't get past Eagle Hill. He'd drop us at the McArdle Bridge. I wanted Geena with us all the way to Jefferies. It was only a mile and a half to the docks, maybe two, but it could be a very long march. Once at the docks I planned to give Geena the news. I wanted to put that off as long as possible. Our flight to the bridge was slow in the low level street-lanes, but we saw no cops. We landed on the south end of Pearl Street.

"The boat's named *Lucky Linda*," Cookie said. "Captain's named Roan. Don't know what pier it is, but when you get to the waterfront people will help. Sailors tend to stick together. Now he won't put to sea till he gets word from me, so just be patient."

"You stay frosty," I said.

"Ice," Cookie said. Then he slammed the car shut and lifted away.

At the end of Pearl there was a buffer zone to the wall that ran Marginal Street. It was all concertina wire and break beams. The Border Patrol really didn't care about people leaving. They didn't get along with the cops, so if there wasn't a price on your head a simple bribe got you across. They scanned our faces, but didn't have retina shooters. Still it was an uneasy few minutes before their machine cleared us. It cost me two hundred. Cheap. On the other side things got hairy.

Once the gates closed behind us, the lights got weird. They went from electric to fire like that. To our right the water lapped the wall. To our left was a dark fenced-in prison or something; lots of raggedy people clustered around fires and doing not much of anything. All along the causeway people were camped and there was a haphazard path winding through to the lifts. We were careful not to trespass.

McArdle was an old draw bridge, long since rusted useless. But the lift works ahead of us was like a fort. There was an arch built up over the road. It looked like it was made of driftwood and twisted rebar all meshed together. There were torches all around it, and I thought I saw skulls in it.

"Spooky," Jane said.

"Cool," the other one said.

"Quiet."

As we approached the arch there was a commotion. Rags piled along the road stirred to life and six people stood holding spears. Someone whistled a strange quick thing and someone from beyond the arch shouted,

"What?"

Another whistle.

"Yer kiddin'."

A third whistle and we heard clattering. Then a thumping sound and all six of the rag-people

76

grabbed torches and lit the arch, and there was an eyeful.

He stood easily eight feet tall and he wore a red skirt that was made of fabrics layered over and over. He was bare from the waist up and he was amazingly muscled. But it looked like his muscles didn't have any skin; just raw and red sinuous stuff. I couldn't tell if it was real or some sort of appliance.

His face was almost the same. He wore a dark half-mask covering his mouth and jaw, but his nose and slanted eyes were raw like his chest. He had two long horns sprouting his temples and dark scraggly hair that fell like a horse's mane. He held a long staff as if it were a punter's pole, and a bronze sword hung by his side.

"Whaaa . . . ?" I said.

"Who would cross the Styx and enter the realm of Hell?" he said, his voice convincingly basso.

"Hi," I said. "I'm Martha and these four are the Tweedle sisters. Who the hell are you?"

"You!" he boomed pointing his staff at us, "must tell me! Speak my name or none shall pass."

"What?"

"Speak my name or none shall pass!"

"Rumpelstiltskin?"

"There Charon stands," Jane sang.

"He who rules the dreary coast," the other harmonized.

"A sordid god."

"And I can't remember the rest."

"Neither can I."

"Mondo cool," the man said, nodding. His minions were also impressed. "You guys like scholars or something?"

"Or something," Jane said.

"Unfortunately,"

"oh, wafter of souls,"

"we forgot our pennies,"

"but we got a bunch of Nollyoaty bars!"

"That'll do." the beast said.

Candy was passed all about, and great Charon granted us entrance to Hell Town.

Across the bridge it wasn't all that bad. I mean for a place that had no electricity, water or sewer, people were doing something to carve out a life. A lot of houses and buildings were still intact. We saw chicksens, or gees or something like them in yards, and a lot of homes had firelight inside. People were on the road, a lot on bicycles, but they all kept to themselves and made no eye-contact. An occasional police drone would fly by, but none of them ever stopped to look at anything. Way off to our left we saw a section of the skyline backlit with orange.

We crossed London Street and passed over the service road to the old airport. There was a line of trees flanking the road on either side. And then there was another. And then it got eerie. It seemed darker, and the further south we went there were fewer and fewer people on the road, and those we saw walked or biked in groups. Then the houses there were empty. And it got quiet.

At that point Geena and I took our holsters from out packs, strapped them on and charged the pistols. Beneath their ponchos and leggings the Janes wore the cop's armor. They pocketed their guns. Shelly looked so timid and frightened. We kept her in the middle. The first sign of trouble was when we saw the barricade and fires down on Maverick Square.

"Wait here," Geena said.

She leapt to the fire escape of a gutted brick building and climbed to the roof. She had a scanner and she cased the area.

"No good," she said when she returned. "We're hemmed in by collapsed and smoldering buildings. There's two barricades overlapping, and a path between. Bunch of people, I counted six but there's heat everywhere along the barricade and all over in the buildings. It looks like a toll."

"That makes sense," I said. "But I don't like it. I don't like it at all. All we got is money and us, and it's a sure thing that they have no use for money here. We double back and find another way."

"Absolutely."

We backed away. If they saw us from the blockade or not, we didn't know. My thought was to strike for the river and make our way off the road. Geena agreed. But we hadn't gone half a block when hell began to break loose.

From nowhere a rocket screamed in and tore into the barricade. The concussion sent us all to the ground. Then there was screaming and then there was roaring. Motorcycles tore down from the north, and shots were fired from the buildings all around us. Cop drones filled the air. Smaller rockets whizzed past and grenades exploded in the buildings. The bikes zoomed past us. Three were picked off and crashed. The barricade was blown to cinders. I heard yelling and people began to fill the street and square. There was firing and there were swords while the drones took pot-shots at the combatants. We were in the middle of a frigging war.

"Move!" Geena shouted.

We got to our feet and followed her down an alley. Shots chased us. Something punched the armor on my shoulder and I sprawled to the ground. The Janes stopped, turned and fired. The shots ended. I climbed to my feet.

"Shelly's down!"

"Tante!"

Geena scooped her up. We flew out and into a dark street. The combat was behind us. We raced through an empty warehouse that opened into the river. We jumped in. The current was slow but strong, the tide was drawing out. I snapped on my helmet and switched on the light. The others found me and we huddled tight. The water was foul.

"Shelly?" I ask, near frantic.

"I don't know," Geena said.

She had the woman across her back holding her arms around her shoulders. Shelly's head was down.

"Tante Shelly," the Janes wailed.

"Quiet damn it!"

We heard the war raging not a few hundred yards to our left, but the river carried us away. It got quieter and it got darker. I heard the twins weeping. We pumped our legs struggling to stay close to the shore. There were shadows of derelict buildings there. We floated.

80

Then we bumped something in the dark and were whirled around a huge piling. There we saw light; real electric light.

As one we began to wave and shout for help. From one pier there was movement. Then a light played the water till it found us. We called out frantically. They threw us a life line with a single ring. I snagged it and we were pulled to a small pontoon. Hands helped us out of the water. I heard the twins cough and sputter. I dropped my helmet and just collapsed, water cascading from my suit.

"What the hell do we got here?" someone said.

"I dunno," another answered. "But this one's dead."

My heart stopped.

"No" I said softly. "No. No. She can't – Shelly?"

I crawled to her. She lay on her back. Her eyes were open as though she were gazing at the stars that weren't there. She looked so calm.

But I wasn't. I grabbed her. I cradled her in my arms.

"Shelly," I said. "It's okay now. We made it. We're safe."

A strange gurgling came from her throat.

"Shelly please."

I felt the warmth trickling from her back. From the corner of my eye I saw the red swelling onto the deck.

"Shelly baby? Please . . . Pleeeeaseeeeee!"

9 - Escape

The sea was ashen grey and rolling. We were hours beyond the twelve mile limit and on serious open water. A hazy dawn was taking the sky ahead of us. *Lucky Linda's* name held. The Coast Guard had scanned us and waved us on, and while the sea tossed and swelled it wasn't anything the ship couldn't handle. I sat topside huddled in a blanket and nestled in a big coil of rope. Geena and the girls were below. I couldn't look at them.

It was very hard for me to not hate myself.

If it weren't for me, Shelly wouldn't have died in such a meaningless way. I dragged her along through Hell because I wanted Geena covering my back. I should have left the two with Cookie. I should have shoved Geena's papers in Shelly's hand and sent them back to Amnesty. They were bright. They'd have figured out a way and Shelly would still be . . . alive.

And after all that the girl had gone through in her life . . . just getting through school and colony rating was an accomplishment for a kid with her background. Then there was Uptown. Then there was her Friday, and then her stomach thing. By all accounts she should have chucked all and taken a nice cushy admin job with the government.

But no, she was a flipping angel. She signed on with Amnesty and worked with countless kids like the Janes or worse. And she got killed being their mother-hen. And the worst part was that it didn't count for anything. She wasn't even a part of whatever it was those moron bangers were fighting about. It was all so senseless. And it was my fault.

Sometime after it had all sank in, back on the pier, and they had pried my baby from my arms, I remember hearing someone muttering a prayer. I wanted to spit. I looked up and saw the twins huddling together and weeping like babies, and at that moment it was so very hard for me not to loathe them. At that awful moment I blamed them, and I hated them and their annoying cutsie way of talking and their stupid questions and their ugly faces with their double eyebrows, their doe eyes and those silly horns that were probably implants anyway.

But looking at them, seeing and sharing their grief, I knew better. In my rational mind I knew that it wasn't their fault. I knew that they were innocents swept up in a thing that they had nothing to do with. They just wanted a chance to grow up somewhere and get in trouble all on their own. And I tried really hard not to hate them for all of this.

It took a while for the fishermen to sort things out. My brain was numb. Geena stepped up and made them understand. They were all smugglers anyway. They took us to Roan and his boat, and Geena did the negotiations. I don't know what the bribe cost me and I didn't care. I knew that she helped persuade him and I didn't care about that either, as long as she didn't get some disease. I don't even remember getting under way. I just knew that I shouldn't be near the twins. So as soon as we cleared the Coast Guard I grabbed a blanket and went on deck. Sometime, somebody handed me a hot cup of coffee. It went cold in my hands.

"Oh shit," I said to the misty disk of the sun. "I don't even know what they did with her body."

"I made a small donation," Geena said softly, "to the Fisherman's Widow's Fund. They're going to take care of her. They promised a church and everything."

"A church?"

"It's what they do."

I wanted to spit.

Instead I spilled my coffee, fell into my Geena's arms and cried like a baby.

Everyone always talks about the romance of the sea. For me it was boring. There was nothing but the same for miles and miles and miles. Same color, same rollers, same rocking, same little boat and nowhere to go. Roan and his crew were working, and I tried to stay out of their way. That put me in the bow of the ship where I mindlessly watched the prow plow through the waves.

It was hypnotic after a while, and I needed that. I had to put Shelly out of my mind because there were a few more things to do before I could grieve. The twins were the first and obvious problem, but barring anything going wrong on Cookie's end, they would soon be safe in Montana somewhere. The plan was for me to join them, but I would need to think about that later. My real problem was Geena.

She shouldn't have been with us. She should have been with Shelly making their way back to New Haven. What was I supposed to do when Cookie showed up? His lander was only a three seater and the twins were going to have to share one.

I had a vague notion that I should tell her to meet me in Helena. That would give her a direction, and she'd figure out a way. But there were so many holes in that one. If she ever got caught without her owner she'd be sent back to the Farm. And even if I gave her her papers my name would pop up as a fugitive and she'd be sent back to the Farm. And that was the one thing that terrified her most. I saw her looking at me a lot, and I knew that she knew what I was thinking.

The fishermen had baited their last hook when Roan came up to me and told me that Cookie was on his way and should pop up real soon. It was decision time. I scanned the skies. I saw nothing, but it was overcast and I didn't know which direction he'd come from. Then Roan tapped my shoulder and pointed to starboard.

At first it looked like the water was doming, then it started churning and then the long orca-tube with gently rounded stingray wings broke the surface alongside the Luck Linda. The ship's crew lowered a long gang plank as the lander's hatch slid open. Cookie fastened it and I watched two cloaked and hooded figures scramble across. The crew escorted them below and a moment later Geena led the twins topside. Cookie pointed to me and waved me to come aboard.

"Geena," I said. "Come with me please."

"Yes mistress."

In the cramped cockpit there were two seats forward and one behind. As soon as we sat Cookie said,

"Captain Roan has informed me of events, and I am very sorry for your loss. From what little I saw, I saw that she was a good and caring woman."

"Thank you."

"But," he went on. "There is news. The Western Preserve is shut down. There's an outbreak of Dengue in the Middle Province and Helena's pulled the hatch."

I felt my stomach drop.

"Dengue?" I said.

"Yes."

"Your crew?"

"Indefinite quarantine."

"Oh Nathan."

"I am a gentleman, Ms. Waters or Teasdale or whoever the hell you are, and it is that gentlemanly nature that is respecting your grieving, and keeping me from busting your teeth out."

I sat speechless. I had never felt lower or more worthless in my life. My brain refused to function and I simply could not think. Again Geena stepped up.

"Captain Cook," she said. "Your troubles are hard, but they are temporary. If you are indeed a gentleman you will help us turn our thought to the two girls. They are innocents and for their sake alone we must think of something fast."

"Yeah," he said with a sigh. "That thought did cross my mind. Ain't no place on earth I can think of but . . . there's always L-3."

86

That slapped my brain. L-3 was a start-up colony, and like L-4 and 5, it was on the same orbital plane; good clean goldilocks sunshine. And as a fledgling colony, they'd open their arms to a couple of teenage savants. No smuggling.

"If they'll go," he said.

"They'll go," I said. "They'll go where ever their Tante Geena takes them."

"Mistress?"

"That's all there is too it," I said. "There is no room on this ship for the both of us, so you are taking my place."

"Mistress no."

"Geena, you can't say no to me. Besides you wouldn't last a week alone and without papers and without a home in Boston. You'd be back at the Farm in no time."

"And you could?" she said. "You could last with the police, Phelps' people and Alistair looking for you?"

"I can make something work in Hell town."

"Are there a lot of touch-heads in Hell town?" she asked. "You wouldn't last a month, mistress. You cannot stay, and I cannot stay. So it's settled. I'll ride in the hold."

"You'll freeze!"

"I'll shut down."

"But this guy's got a drop in Moscow," I said. "What are they gonna think about a cute little blonde all balled up and rolling around in their chili?"

"Chili?"

"Um. Ladies," Cookie said. "I got hidey hole back there. It's pressurized, but it is freezing."

"I can last two days below zero," Geena said.

"No," I said. "It's too dangerous. This thing has to fly to Moscow. The acceleration – the deceleration – you'll bounce all over the place. Something could go wrong and the hold could lose pressure; I see that all the time. Geena, if something happened to you I couldn't live with myself if I was responsible for losing someone else I loved."

"Mistress?"

"Oh—just stay in that chair, damn it," I snapped. "I'm staying. I'm going to get the twins."

Her hand clamped my shoulder. It was like iron holding me.

"Captain," Geena said. "Kindly drop your gentlemanly nature a moment, would you please?"

Cookie punched my lights out.

10 - The May Queen

I wasn't out long, but it was enough. The hatch was shut, the twins were strapped in the aft chair and I was belted down tight. It felt as if we were floating.

"Sure, you can do it," Cookie was saying as my brain cleared. "Which one?"

"Me, me!" Jane said.

"No me!" the other one cried.

"I'll choose," Cookie said. "Eenie, meenie, miney –you!"

"Coowell!"

"Okay now," he said. "Ready, steady . . ."

One of the twins reached forward and touched a green button.

"Go!"

I heard a click. There was a second and then it was like an explosion. I was slammed back in my seat. The twins squealed. I heard a roaring and felt a rattling. More and more it was like I was being crushed. My chest felt heavy and I thought that my ribs would squash my lungs and heart. Even my cheeks were plastered against my skull.

But even as the acceleration nailed me, we broke through the clouds and I was suddenly flooded with awe. The sun was a brilliant yellow, so bright that I couldn't look at it. The sky was a dazzling blue and clean and crisp just like the books imagined. As we rose the blue deepened to azure and then to purple, and away above I saw the black of night. I swore that I saw stars. Even the Janes were quiet.

The weight on my chest eased slowly. I began to feel normal. Then I felt lighter than normal and then I was floating, only the straps keeping me in my seat. We drifted like that, suspended between sky and space. The stars I saw began to creep ever so slowly.

This was nothing like the blind needle ships I'd ride to the station. That was not an automatic elevator that went from one coordinate to another guided by computers and designed to give no sensation of motion.

This was – this was flying.

"Six minutes up," Cookie said, "six minutes cruising, and forty minutes down."

I looked at him.

"You did it," I said. "Didn't you? She's back there, isn't she?"

"She insisted."

"She dies, I'll kill you."

"Sammie—"

"Jessie."

"Whoever. Enjoy the view."

"Those are real stars?" a Jane asked.

The view was so splendid. The greatest thing was that it looked so clean. There was no haze, no mist, nothing dirty or spoiled. It was pristine and it slowly moved above us like something ever so vast and ever so eternal.

And then I felt something tug me.

"Hang on," Cookie said.

Weight began the return. The nose of the lander dipped slowly, and I saw the curve of the planet swathed in white. It looked so pretty from above.

But as it loomed larger and larger I got heavier and heavier. It wasn't half as bad as the up-ride, but when we plunged into those clouds that was all we saw for a while.

The motion in my guts told me that we were moving, but nothing that I could see gave any hint of that. It was a constant grey until we slowed. Then little beads of water began to trail across the windows. Then a city formed through the mist ahead. It was concentric circles built around a winding river. We bumped a little and then I saw traffic. We were in a lane.

We got a slot quickly. The Ruskies are known for their efficiency. We parked and we were surrounded by soldiers with guns. I gaped, Cookie waved. Someone waved back. Then the radio started talking and Cookie spoke in Russian. It sounded light. He flipped a switch and the trunk in the back popped open. It took them twenty minutes to unload the chili. The scanners gave the ship a once over and then the soldiers left.

"I love the Ruskies," Cookie said. "So no nonsense."

"Who'd you bribe?"

"Commissar Antonio Roberto DaSilva," he said. "Cinco de Mayo is coming."

I laughed for the first time in a long while.

The hold was then loaded with pure, sweet Russian Vodka. The good stuff.

We were in and out of Moscow in record time. We circled in the eject lane another half hour, and then we took another bone wrenching ride up into low orbit. I kept thinking of Geena.

Weightless and seemingly drifting, Cookie assured us that we were indeed on a course to rendezvous with Up Station Nine. The Janes gaped and gazed in wonder asking a thousand questions that Cookie happily answered. Inside of an hour the station came into view. The sun was behind us, and the station seemed to materialize as a glittering spiked gem. I was surprised at how quickly it formed in our view.

"Something's wrong," Cookie said.

"What?"

"I can't raise port authority."

"Are you line-of-sight?" I asked. "Maybe your—"

"I'm on ELF. Nothing."

The station was a haphazard sort of thing. It had started a long time ago as an Earth-International collaborative and the basic structure just kept getting added onto until it became that sprawling, bristling hodgepodge of a Customs and Inspection Port. There were brilliant parts and dark parts and there were some parts on our left that were glowing orangey blue.

"What the flup?" Cookie said.

"What is it?"

"Fire."

"You can't have a fire in space," a Jane said.

"The composites that make the exo-frame have oxygen," Cookie said. "The skin's burning."

The blue glow was eating away at a large pod to our starboard.

"Can we get to the *May Queen*?" I asked.

"Oh we can dock alright; got no choice in the matter now. Isaac Newton says so. But if I can't raise anybody I can't get clearance. We can't cut the moorings. We'll be stuck."

"See if," I said, thinking. "See if you can raise the Bureau on board."

I gave him the freek. He punched it in. we heard a soft, charmingly calm voice.

". . . has been declared. Protocol four is in effect. Go immediately to your safe-place. Repeat: An Emergency has been declared . . ."

"Shit."

"What happened?"

"Damned if I know."

The lander's course took us out of sight of the fire. We were in shadow. There were no mooring lights, no beacons, nothing.

"Power's out," Cookie said. "Brace yourselves!"

In the darkness ahead we saw a slit of light grow broader and brighter. It was the *May Queen's* shuttle dock. It was a lone warm glow in a sea of silent black. The ship had sensed its baby, and we were being guided home by momma. We slowly entered the deck and it was a comfort to see. The lander touched down light as a feather.

"That wasn't so bad," I said relaxing.

"Hold on!"

Suddenly we were jolted forward and then we were slammed. The lander skidded, and I watched in terror as the ship's bulkhead loomed. Then in an instant the windows went white and we slammed to a jarring stop. The only thing that kept me from plowing into the dash were the restraints.

"Everybody okay?" Cookie called.

"Geena!" I said.

The white on the windows disappeared and I saw red lights flashing and heard a claxon raging.

"What happened?" Jane cried.

"Are we okay?" her sister yelled.

"We've got to get Geena!"

"Sit tight!" Cookie said. "Everybody! We don't move till the deck is pressurized."

"What just happened?"

"Power on the station is out?" he answered. "Isaac Newton."

Without power the moorings and buffers stabilizing the *May Queen* were down. That was just fine as everything was in a state of inertia, the whole of the complex rotating together. But when the lander came in, the last vestiges of its momentum was transferred to the ship, which in turn began to move. The object in motion hit the object at rest, and the result was a collision. The *May Queen's* safety overrides blew out a buffer that kept the lander from ramming through the bulkhead. But the whole ship itself was thrust forward into the station.

"Air bags," Cookie said. "I just hope that the station's docking emergency runs on batteries."

The wailing from outside stopped, but the red lights kept flashing.

"We got air," Cookie said. "Popping the hood."

Outside the lander there was no gravity. The Janes had no idea what to do and were totally adrift and out of control. Cookie and I ignored them. We flew to the hold and opened the compartment.

Geena was curled up tight in a ball and enmeshed in strapping. She was blue and covered with frost. She looked like she took a few bruises but I didn't see any red. That was something. But we couldn't know if she was injured until she woke herself. And to do that she needed warmth, and gravity. We eased her out and into the landing dock.

"Tante Geena," Jane cried.

"Is she okay?"

The twins had already figured out freefall and zoomed to us. We were working Geena and ourselves to the shaft that led to the living quarters when the claxons shrieked again. I near jumped out of my skin.

"Fire," Cookie said. "Let's move."

We drifted as fast as we could. We made it to the living quarters. It was lit and warm, but not rotating. Cookie ordered the Janes to stay put with Geena. He dragged me forward to the wheel house and slammed me into the co-pilot's seat. There were a thousand buttons and screens and controls I didn't understand. Outside the huge window I saw nothing. Monitors snapped on and there was a view of blue fire eating at black, and it was getting closer. He didn't need to tell me what it was.

And then I felt motion.

"Shit!"

"What?" I cried.

"They cut this pod off the station," he said. "We're drifting."

"They abandoned—"

"Watch those numbers," he said pointing to a slender screen. "Every fifty digits press that blue button and turn this one click."

"What—"

"Just flipping do it."

I glued my eyes. The readout was rising. When it hit fifty I did my job, and the numbers got faster every time. Cookie was going crazy reaching all around the controls.

"When it reaches five-hundred," he said, "yellow button."

"Can you tell me what's going on?"

"My ship uses airbags," he said calmly. "The station uses foam, and that creates a cocoon. We are wrapped, and I gotta break out of that without ripping the nose off."

"Oh."

"And the fun part is that if the magnet moorings still have emergency power they're gonna spark when I break 'em."

"Not good?"

"The foam's got oxygen."

"Oh."

"We'll never know what hit us," he said, shrugging.

"Five hundred!" I cried, punching the yellow button

He sat back. He took a breath and flipped a toggle. He gripped the chair arms.

"May the road rise to meet us," he said.

I felt a big jolt, and then slow motion. From the monitor I saw blue fire close. Very close. Then I saw a flash, and Cookie winced. I could almost hear

96

soft tearing sounds, then I could feel them. There was another flash and then another and Cookie's knuckles turned white. My heart was in my throat—

And then there was a huge white flash from the dark windows and then we were tumbling. I screamed. Cookie whooped. We were going end over end and the window went back to black. I was getting dizzy and my stomach traded places with my heart in my throat. But Cookie was laughing and playing monkey again with his controls. The roll slowly nulled.

"That was fun," he said, as we stabilized.

"What happened?"

"We got lucky," he said. "There was enough strain on the foam so that when the last moorings sparked the flash tore it free. Most of the blaze stayed dockside."

"Most?"

"Yeah, I should do something about that."

He opened a panel and after snapping some switches took up a joystick. Another monitor blinked to life. I saw stars. Then a light snapped on and I saw the ship's bow. The bulbous capsule was enveloped in yellowy foam that stretched out for almost a hundred yards. At the tip of the foam blue fire was eating toward us.

"Like I said," he said, "most."

I saw a drone drift into view.

"Can you—"

"Yes."

The drone drove to a place just forward of the ship's prow. A small beam appeared and slashed the elongated foam in two places. The ship drifted away from them by inches, but both sections still followed. The blue fire ate its way down the trailing section all the way to the cut. Then it went out. Cookie let out a breath, then sliced another piece off for good measure. As the drone backed away we got a good look at the ship. It was, to say the least ridiculous looking.

"Should rename this thing the *Condom*," Cookie chuckled.

The view aft showed the living section starting to rotate. Cookie snapped on the com.

"Hey Jane and Jane," he called. "All is well. Gravity's on its way. Hunker down somewhere you two. I'm setting course--"

"Geena!" they cried. "It's Geena! Something horrible has happened! Help! Help!"

I flew.

By the time I got to them Geena was thawed but only half uncurled, and her head was not her head.

"Alistair," I said.

"Evening, Jessie-dog," he smiled, "and congratulations. You found my girls. Good job. Happy Friday."

"Alistair," I said, taking a breath, "I've changed my mind."

"I thought that you might. And so I'm going to give you one more chance. You see sweetie, you're a real wanted woman. Not only did you kill a bunch of cops—"

"You killed them."

"That's not the way Boston PD sees it," he said. "And, add to that the two Phelps operatives you nailed."

98

"That was self-defense."

"That's not the way Interpol sees it. And trying to burn down a Station Pod to cover your tracks?"

"You son of a bitch."

"Like I say, you're a real wanted woman downside. There's no place on the planet you can go. And the way I figure it in about a week or two you're going to need another fix of angel tears. Are there a lot of touch-heads up on the *May Queen*?"

I didn't answer.

"Your only hope is me, girl. I am within range. Come to me and all will be forgiven."

"Bullshit."

"Don't make me call out the flying monkeys."

"Geena, end transmission."

Her head went fuzzy and then she slumped. The Janes cradled her. In a moment our Geena was back. Her eyes fluttered open and she started to uncurl.

"Tante Geena,"

"are you alright?"

"My head hurts," she said stretching out on the floor. "And I feel all knotted up. Where are we? What day is it?"

"It ain't Friday," I said.

The End